RAVENSCROFT

Laura Shenton

RAVENSCROFT

Laura Shenton

Iridescent Toad Publishing

Iridescent Toad Publishing.

Cover by Art Lynx Covers.

First edition. ISBN 978-1-913779-21-4

Chapter One

The deli counter smelt like despair and yesterday's fried chicken. Brianna – or Brie, as she preferred – stood behind the glass case, her chin resting on her palm. Her green hair was a rebellion against the store's drab uniform, tied back in a messy bun with stray strands falling into her eyes. She flicked them aside, glaring at the rows of potato salads and cold cuts that glistened under the unforgiving fluorescent lights.

"I said thin slices, not whatever that is," snapped the woman in front of her.

Brie blinked, shifting her gaze to the shrivelled customer holding a plastic-wrapped abomination of turkey slices.

"It's turkey," Brie said, her voice flat.

"It's uneven!" the woman screeched, slapping the package onto the counter as though she was submitting evidence in a courtroom drama. "You call this service? My cat wouldn't eat this!"

Brie rolled her eyes. "Well, your cat's taste is questionable."

"Excuse me?"

"Oh, nothing," Brie said sweetly, flashing a saccharine smile. Her fingers twitched behind the counter, itching for a little spellwork. The last thing she wanted to do was argue with a Karen about sandwich meat, but the universe, in its infinite cruelty, had trapped her here for eight hours a day.

The woman launched into a tirade about respect and customer service, words that flowed over Brie like rain on a waxed car. Brie let her rant, her mind wandering to the potion bottles she'd left on her kitchen counter. A new brew she was testing – something for headaches, though it smelt more like burnt popcorn – hadn't quite set. She made a mental note to fix it when she got home.

"And another thing," the woman said, jabbing a finger at Brie, "if I ever see this kind of incompetence again, I'll be speaking to your manager."

The manager. Brie glanced over her shoulder at Carl, the manager in question, visible through the slightly ajar door of his office at the back. A balding man who spent most of his day scrolling through his phone, he wouldn't save her. He never did.

That was when Brie decided she'd had enough.

"Of course, madam," she said, her voice syrupy and false. "Let me fix that for you."

The woman huffed, arms crossed as she waited for Brie to somehow fix everything, as if that were even possible. Brie, however, had other plans. Under the counter, she discreetly traced a small sigil in the air with her finger. Her magic was simple, subtle – no grand gestures, no glowing lights. A faint shimmer flickered in the air, gone in a blink.

Brie picked up the knife and began cutting the meat into smaller pieces, though she knew it was pointless. There was no way it could be sliced thinner now. Still, she went through the motions, her movements automatic and detached – a hollow gesture made more for show than out of any real effort to please. She didn't care; the customer wouldn't be satisfied no matter what she did, so why bother?

"There," Brie said, handing back the package of turkey.

The woman opened the package, her brow furrowing as she inspected its contents. Her lips pursed in disapproval, and she plucked out a small piece of meat, holding it up to the light as if expecting to find fault. Finally, she took a tentative bite, her face twisting almost instantly. "What is this? It tastes like... nail polish!"

"Strange," Brie said, feigning concern. "Must be the supplier."

The woman's face flushed with anger as she stormed off, shouting about reporting the store to corporate. Brie leaned back against the counter, smirking.

"Another happy customer," she muttered.

From the corner of her eye, Brie noticed Carl watching her, his phone lowered for the first time that day. His brow furrowed, and he mouthed the words, "My office. Now."

Brie groaned. She pulled off her gloves and apron, tossing them onto the counter, and trudged towards the back. The day couldn't get worse – could it?

Carl's office smelt like stale coffee. Brie slumped into the chair across from his desk, crossing her arms and glaring at the motivational posters on the wall. "Hang in there," said a kitten clinging to a branch. Brie considered setting the poster on fire with a well-aimed spell, just for entertainment.

Carl cleared his throat, drawing her attention. He was middle-aged and perpetually tired, with a comb-over that was losing its battle against time. He stared at her like a principal preparing to scold a problem student.

"Brie," he began, his voice heavy with fake sympathy. "You're a good worker when you try."

"You think?" Brie said sarcastically, arching a brow.

Carl ignored her. "But you have an attitude problem. Customers are complaining – again."

"Oh, really?" Brie feigned shock. "Do they have a problem with me existing, or is it my ability to slice turkey at an angle that doesn't satisfy their delicate sensibilities?"

"Come on, Brie!" Carl said with a sigh, slumping back in his chair and rubbing his temples. He slapped a hand on the desk, though it lacked any real force, more a gesture of frustration than intimidation. "You're on thin ice. I mean it this time. One more incident, and I'll have no choice but to fire you."

"Oh no, not that," Brie deadpanned. "What will I ever do without this fulfilling career?"

Carl glared at her, his face turning red. "I'm serious, Brie. You..."

But before he could finish, the office door burst open.

Three figures stepped in, their presence impossible to ignore. They were dressed in dark robes, their faces obscured by shadowy hoods. The air around them crackled with restrained energy, and Brie's stomach sank. She recognised them immediately – the Magic Council.

Carl blinked, confused. "Uh... can I help you?"

One of the robed figures stepped forward, ignoring Carl entirely. "Brianna Holloway?"

Brie sat up straighter, her sass evaporating under the weight of their collective gaze. "Maybe," she said cautiously.

"You are charged with violating the Code of Magical Conduct," the lead figure announced, their voice cold and authoritative. "Specifically, misuse of magic against a civilian."

Brie's eyes widened. "You've got to be kidding me."

Carl looked between Brie and the council members, his mouth opening and closing like a fish. "Wait, what's going on? What are you talking about?"

"Stay out of this, mortal," snapped one of the other figures, waving a hand dismissively.

Carl fell silent, too shocked to say anything back.

Brie groaned, throwing her hands up. "Ok, listen, it wasn't that big of a deal. That lady was a nightmare, and I just… made her food taste bad. Big whoop."

"The Code exists for a reason," the lead figure said, their tone icy. "Magic is not to be used frivolously, regardless of the provocation. Your actions could have escalated dangerously."

"Oh please," Brie scoffed. "She was fine. She'll probably complain to someone about her taste buds and move on. Nobody's dead."

"Enough," the figure interrupted, their patience clearly wearing thin. "You will accompany us to Ravenscroft for disciplinary action. Effective immediately."

"Ravenscroft?" Brie asked, frowning. "What is that, some kind of magical detention centre?"

The lead figure didn't answer. Instead, they raised a hand, and Brie felt the air around her tighten, magic coiling around her like invisible ropes. She struggled, her protests muffled by the spell.

"Come quietly," the figure said. "Or we'll make this harder than it needs to be."

Brie glared at them but ultimately relented, slumping in her chair. "Fine," she said. "But for the record, this is a total overreaction."

The lead figure didn't respond. With a flick of their wrist, a portal opened in the centre of the room, swirling with dark energy. Brie stared at it, her stomach twisting.

"Well, this day officially sucks," she muttered as they dragged her through.

Chapter Two

Brie stumbled as she emerged from the portal, the swirling vortex spitting her out onto damp cobblestones. She barely had time to register her surroundings before the portal snapped shut behind her with a resounding *crack*, leaving her in eerie silence.

She straightened, brushing off her jeans and glaring at the three robed figures who had escorted her. "A little warning next time, huh? My lunch almost came back up."

"Silence!" the lead figure barked.

Brie made a face but didn't argue. Instead, she took in the towering structure before her. Ravenscroft loomed like something out of a gothic horror novel – a sprawling old manor surrounded by mist-shrouded woods.

The jagged spires reached into the grey sky like skeletal fingers, and the stone walls seemed to hum faintly with latent magic.

"Cheery," Brie muttered.

The robed figures ignored her and motioned for her to walk. One stepped ahead, while the other two flanked her sides, positioning themselves just close enough to block any escape attempts. Not that there was anywhere to run, Brie realised with a sinking feeling. She was guided up a narrow path lined with glowing sigils etched into the ground. They pulsed faintly as she stepped over them, and she could feel the faint thrum of magic beneath her feet.

As they approached the massive double doors, they swung open with a slow, ominous creak. Inside, the air was thick with the scent of old books and candle wax. The entrance hall was cavernous, its walls lined with portraits of scowling witches. Their eyes seemed to follow Brie as she walked.

"Creepy and judgmental," she remarked, glancing at one particularly sour-looking witch. "Feels like home already."

The lead figure came to a halt in the centre of the hall, turning to face her. "You will wait here," they commanded.

Brie crossed her arms. "Sure, I'll just stand here and think about my life choices."

The figure ignored her sarcasm and disappeared through a side door, leaving her alone with the other two robed council members. They stood like statues, silent and imposing, and Brie found herself tapping her foot just to break the oppressive quiet.

It wasn't long before the side door creaked open again, and a new figure stepped out. She was tall and severe, her black robes trimmed with deep crimson. Her sharp features were framed by streaks of grey in her otherwise dark hair, and her piercing eyes seemed to see right through Brie.

"I am Madam Delacroix, headmistress of this academy," the woman said, her voice as sharp as her appearance. "Welcome to Ravenscroft."

"Thanks, I hate it," Brie replied without missing a beat.

Madam Delacroix raised an eyebrow, unimpressed. "Your reputation precedes you, Miss Holloway. Reckless. Disrespectful. A tendency to flout the rules."

"Wow, my résumé's really making the rounds," Brie said, smirking.

"You are here because the Magic Council has deemed you a danger to society," Madam Delacroix continued, ignoring her. "Ravenscroft exists to correct such behaviours. You will learn discipline, responsibility, and control – or you will face expulsion. And trust me, Miss Holloway, expulsion from Ravenscroft is not something you want."

Brie arched a brow. "What, you send people to magical prison or something?"

Madam Delacroix smiled thinly. "Let's just say the consequences are... permanent."

The air in the hall seemed to grow colder, and Brie's smirk faltered. For the first time, she began to wonder if she might be in over her head.

"Your orientation begins immediately," Madam Delacroix said. She gestured to one of the council members, who handed Brie a small, leather-bound handbook. The cover was embossed with the academy's crest – a raven perched on a gnarled branch.

"What's this?" Brie asked, flipping it open.

"Your rulebook," Madam Delacroix said. "Study it well. Every infraction adds time to your sentence here."

Brie groaned. "Great. Homework already."

Madam Delacroix ignored her and gestured towards a staircase at the far end of the hall. "Your quarters have been prepared. One of our students will show you around."

As if on cue, a figure emerged from the shadows – a young woman with long, wild, dark curls framing her face, and a mischievous grin. She wore the academy uniform, though her version looked far from pristine. The robe hung loosely off one shoulder, revealing a scruffy, thick, black jumper underneath that was clearly not standard issue. Her boots were scuffed, the laces uneven. The overall effect was one of casual rebellion.

"Melinda Sharpe," the girl introduced herself, extending a hand to Brie. "Resident troublemaker and your new best friend."

Brie hesitated for a moment before shaking her hand. "Brie Holloway. Resident sarcastic misfit."

Melinda's grin widened. "Oh, you'll fit right in."

***

Melinda led Brie up the grand staircase, their footsteps echoing through the cavernous space. The higher they climbed, the more the academy seemed to come alive. Candles floated in mid-air, their flames flickering without a breeze. Bronze statues, tarnished and dulled with age, turned their heads to follow the pair as they passed. Brie felt the weight of a hundred unseen eyes, and she couldn't tell if it was creepy or just another part of the academy's over-the-top aesthetic.

"Let me guess," Brie said, glancing at

Melinda. "You're my tour guide because nobody else wanted to babysit the new girl?"

Melinda laughed, a sharp, infectious sound. "Pretty much. Madam Delacroix thinks I'm "a bad influence", so she probably figured sticking me with you would be poetic justice."

"Sounds like we're off to a great start," Brie quipped.

"Don't worry," Melinda said, her grin widening. "You'll love it here. Well, "love" might be a strong word. Let's say you'll learn to tolerate it."

They reached the top of the stairs, where a long corridor stretched before them. The walls were lined with doors, each bearing a small brass plaque with a name etched into it. Melinda stopped in front of one and pushed it open.

"Home sweet home," she said, gesturing for Brie to enter.

The room was small but not terrible. A narrow bed was pushed against one wall, and a wooden desk sat beneath a window that overlooked the misty grounds. A wardrobe stood in the corner, and a small bookshelf was bolted to the wall. Brie noticed the faint scent of lavender in the air, likely from the candle on the desk.

"Well," Brie said, tentatively positioning herself on the edge of the bed, "at least it's not a dungeon."

"Not yet," Melinda quipped. "Stick around long enough, and you might get promoted to one."

Brie snorted. "What's the deal with this place, anyway? I mean, I get that it's supposed to be some kind of reform school for witches, but why does it feel like I'm stuck in some dark, twisted fairytale?"

Melinda plopped onto the bed, her curls bouncing as she flopped backwards. "Ravenscroft has been around forever. It's where the Magic Council sends witches who don't play by their rules. Think of it as a finishing school, but for people like us. Some of us call it "Academy for the Bad". Kind of says it all, doesn't it?"

""People like us?"" Brie echoed, raising an eyebrow.

"Troublemakers," Melinda said with a wink. "We're the ones who don't fit into their neat little boxes. The council doesn't like witches who make waves, so they dump us here and hope we shape up."

"What happens if we don't?" Brie asked, her mind racing.

Melinda hesitated, her playful demeanour slipping for a moment. "Let's just say you don't want to find out."

The weight of the words hung in the air, and Brie felt a chill run down her spine.

"So," Melinda said, breaking the tension, "you planning on toeing the line, or are you going to join the rest of us delinquents?"

Brie smirked, leaning back on her elbows. "I think you already know the answer to that."

"Good," Melinda said, sitting up and clapping her hands together. "In that case, let me show you the ropes. Rule number one: Don't let Charmina get under your skin."

"Charmina?" Brie asked, frowning.

"Picture a walking, talking perfectionist," Melinda said, rolling her eyes. "Straight A grades, perfect attendance, loves tattling. She's basically our natural enemy."

"Sounds delightful," Brie said dryly.

"Oh, she's a peach," Melinda said, her tone dripping with sarcasm. "But don't worry, she's harmless. Mostly."

A knock on the door interrupted them, and a voice Brie didn't recognise called out, "Curfew in fifteen minutes, ladies!"

Melinda groaned. "I forgot about curfew. That's rule number two: Don't get caught sneaking out after hours. They're strict about it."

Brie raised an eyebrow. "And by "strict", you mean...?"

"Detention in the potion labs," Melinda said, shuddering. "Trust me, you don't want to clean cauldrons for six hours."

"Noted," Brie said, already planning how she could bend that rule without breaking it completely.

"Get some rest," Melinda said, standing and stretching. "Tomorrow's your first day of classes, and take my word for it, you're going to need all the energy you can get."

Brie smirked. "Classes? I thought this was supposed to be punishment, not summer camp."

"Oh, it's punishment, all right," Melinda said, grinning wickedly. "You'll see."

With that, she left, leaving Brie alone in her new room. Brie lay back on the bed, staring up at the ceiling. The faint hum of magic seemed to pulse through the walls, and she couldn't shake the feeling that this place was watching her, waiting to see what she'd do next.

"Ravenscroft," she murmured to herself. "What have I got myself into?"

Chapter Three

Morning at Ravenscroft came with all the subtlety of a lightning strike. A loud gong reverberated through the academy, shaking Brie awake with a start. She groaned, burying her face in the pillow, but the sound didn't let up. It was as if the building itself had conspired to ensure she didn't sleep in.

A sharp knock on her door made her groan louder.

"Get up!" Melinda's voice rang out from behind the door. "First day, remember? You don't want to make a bad impression... well, not yet, anyway."

"Go away," Brie muttered into the pillow.

"I'll drag you out myself if I have to," Melinda threatened.

"Fine!" Brie snapped, kicking off the covers.

She stumbled out of bed, still half-asleep, and threw on the uniform she'd found neatly folded on her desk. Apart from a few subtle accents of silver embroidery, it was all black and topped with a dark robe that felt a little too dramatic for her taste.

"Seriously, a robe?" she muttered as she tied it on. "Who designed this? Dracula?"

When Brie opened the door, Melinda was waiting, already dressed and grinning. "Looking sharp," she said, giving Brie a once-over.

Brie glared at her. "You're way too chipper for someone who got woken up by that gong."

"Oh, you'll get used to it," Melinda said, leading her down the hall. "It's like Stockholm syndrome, but for sleep deprivation."

They joined the throng of students streaming towards the dining hall. The chatter was loud and chaotic, with the occasional spark of magic zipping through the air. Brie dodged a floating apple as they entered the massive room, which was lined with long wooden tables and lit by chandeliers that floated lazily overhead.

"What is this, a school for magical show-offs?" Brie muttered, taking in the scene.

"You're really not a morning person, are you?" Melinda said with a smirk.

They grabbed trays and slid into seats at one of the tables. The food appeared on the plates magically – eggs, toast, sausages, and what Brie hoped was coffee. She took a cautious sip and nearly spat it out.

"This isn't coffee," she said, grimacing. "This is hot bean water pretending to be coffee."

"Welcome to Ravenscroft," Melinda said cheerfully, biting into a piece of toast.

Before Brie could reply, a shadow loomed over their table. She looked up to see a tall girl with long, sleek blonde hair and an expression that screamed teacher's pet.

"Charmina Lovelace," the girl introduced herself, her tone prim and condescending.

"And you must be the new arrival. I could have spotted you a mile away with that green hair. You're clearly not one for keeping a low profile. Brianna, is it?"

"Brie," she corrected, already disliking her.

Charmina sniffed. "I've read your file. Quite the record you've got. You'll fit right in with the delinquents."

"Wow," Brie said, raising her coffee cup in a mock toast. "Thanks for the warm welcome. I feel so loved."

Melinda snickered, but Charmina wasn't amused. "I'm only warning you," she said, her voice cold. "The headmistress won't tolerate your antics. Try to behave yourself, for your own sake."

"Noted," Brie said, waving her off. "Now, if you don't mind, I'm trying to enjoy my breakfast."

Charmina's eyes narrowed, but she said nothing more. She turned on her heel and stalked off, leaving Brie to roll her eyes.

"She's a delight," Brie said, taking a bite of toast.

"Oh, she's just jealous," Melinda said, her voice dripping with mock sympathy. "She's spent her whole life trying to be perfect, and here you come, stealing all the attention without even trying."

Brie smirked. "Guess I'm just naturally charming."

The rest of breakfast passed without incident, and soon the students were filing out, heading to their first classes. Melinda dragged Brie along, chattering about the schedule.

"First up: Magical Theory," she said, pulling out a crumpled piece of parchment that served as their timetable. "It's boring as hell, but the professor's blind as a bat, so you can probably get away with sleeping through it."

"Sold," Brie said, tucking her hands into her robe pockets.

The classroom was just as gloomy as the rest of the academy, with walls lined with dusty bookshelves and an ancient blackboard that looked like it hadn't been cleaned in a century. The professor – a frail old witch with thick glasses – began droning on about magical ethics, and Brie felt her eyelids grow heavy almost immediately.

Melinda wasn't kidding about the boredom.

"Psst," Melinda whispered, nudging her.

"What?" Brie muttered, stifling a yawn.

Melinda grinned, holding up a folded piece of parchment. With a flick of her fingers, she sent it floating across the room, where it landed squarely on Charmina's desk.

Charmina opened it, her expression twisting as she read the message. Brie didn't know what it said, but it was enough to make Charmina glare daggers at them.

Brie snorted, biting back laughter. Maybe this place wouldn't be so bad after all.

***

By the end of the lecture, Brie was ready to burn the Magical Theory textbook and use it as kindling. Everything felt so predictable: long-winded speeches about "the responsible use of magic" and "upholding tradition". The only thing keeping her awake was Melinda's whispered commentary, which was far more entertaining than anything the professor had to say.

"You'd think with all the magic in the world, they'd find a way to make the class interesting," Brie muttered as they left the room, filing into the crowded hallway.

"Don't worry," Melinda said, slinging an arm around Brie's shoulders. "The day gets better – or at least more chaotic. Next up: Spellcraft."

"Let me guess," Brie said dryly. "It's another lecture."

"Not quite," Melinda replied, her grin widening. "This one's hands-on. They give us spells to practice, and we try not to blow anything up. Well, most of us try."

Brie smirked. "Sounds more like it."

The spellcraft classroom was a massive open space, its walls reinforced with shimmering enchantments. Students gathered around long worktables laden with jars of glowing powders, enchanted stones, and other magical paraphernalia. At the front of the room, a wiry man with sharp features and an unsettling smile stood with his arms crossed.

"Welcome, witches," he said, his voice slick and calculating. His gaze lingered on Melinda for a moment, then on Brie, his smile widening. "Ah, a new face. How delightful. I am Professor Eryndor, and I will be guiding you through the art of spellcraft – or, as some of you prefer to call it, "controlled chaos"."

Brie leaned towards Melinda. "Is he always this creepy?"

"Always," Melinda whispered back.

Professor Eryndor clapped his hands, and a stack of parchment appeared on each table. "Today's assignment is a simple spell: elemental manipulation. A bit of fire, a bit of water, maybe some wind if you're feeling adventurous. Nothing too dangerous – unless, of course, you make it dangerous."

He gave them a pointed look, his smile never faltering.

Brie glanced at the instructions on the parchment, which detailed the proper hand movements and incantations for summoning small flames. It seemed straightforward enough. She grabbed a jar of red powder and sprinkled a pinch onto the surface of the table, muttering the spell under her breath.

A spark flared to life, hovering just above her hand.

"Not bad," she said, watching the tiny flame flicker.

Melinda, meanwhile, had conjured a fireball the size of an orange. She grinned mischievously, tossing it from hand to hand like a juggler.

"Ooh, get you!" Brie said, amused.

Melinda laughed. "Come on, live a little." She lobbed the fireball into the air, letting it dissipate into harmless sparks before it could hit the ceiling.

Across the room, a loud *pop* drew their attention. One of the other students had accidentally set their parchment on fire, and Charmina was quick to step in, extinguishing the flames with a flick of her wrist.

"Honestly," Charmina said, glaring at the student, "how hard is it to follow instructions?"

Melinda rolled her eyes. "And there's the golden girl, saving the day."

"Looks like she's got a superiority complex," Brie muttered. "I can see why you're not her number-one fan."

The rest of the class passed without major incident. Brie managed to get through the assignment without any disasters, though she couldn't resist adding a bit of flair to her flame spell, making it dance in a spiral.

Professor Eryndor seemed pleased – or at least as pleased as someone with his permanently unsettling smile could look. "A promising start," he said as the class ended. "Let's hope you can maintain it."

As the students filed out, Melinda leaned closer to Brie. "He says that every time. It's like he's waiting for us to mess up so he can make an example out of someone."

"Let me guess," Brie said, "you've been the example more than once."

Melinda grinned. "You catch on quick."

Chapter Four

The afternoon brought free time, which Brie quickly learned was a double-edged sword. Officially, it was meant for studying and self-reflection. Unofficially, it was when most of the trouble happened.

Melinda dragged her to the common room, a sprawling space with mismatched furniture and a crackling fireplace. A group of students sat around a table, playing what looked like a magical version of poker, while others lounged on the couches, chatting and laughing.

"This is where the fun happens," Melinda said, flopping onto a couch and kicking her feet up on the sturdy wooden coffee table. "If you can call it that."

Brie sat beside her, taking in the restless scene. "So, what's the deal? Are we all just supposed to bond over our mutual disdain for authority?"

"Pretty much," Melinda said. "Although some people take this place far more seriously than others." She nodded towards a group in the corner, where Charmina sat with a few other students, her posture stiff and her expression disapproving.

"They're the "model students"," Melinda said, drawing discreet quote marks in the air with her fingers and lowering her voice to a conspiratorial whisper. "They think if they suck up hard enough, they'll get out of here early."

"Do you think they will?"

"I doubt it. Despite what Charmina might think, she's no better than the rest of us... Now, let's see what kind of trouble we can get into before dinner."

Brie barely had time to process Melinda's words before the door to the common room burst open. A girl with fiery red hair and a panicked expression ran in, clutching a smoking bottle.

"Uh-oh," Melinda said, sitting up straighter. "This should be good."

"Everyone, get down!" the girl shouted, waving the bottle in the air.

"What is that?" Brie asked, frowning.

"Looks like an alchemy experiment gone wrong," Melinda said, grinning. "Classic Lisa."

The girl – apparently named Lisa – hurled the bottle towards the fireplace. It shattered on impact, releasing a puff of thick purple smoke that filled the room in seconds. Students coughed and waved their hands in front of their faces as the smoke swirled around them, crackling with stray sparks of energy.

Brie blinked, trying to clear her vision. When the smoke finally dissipated, she realised that the room had changed. The walls were now covered in glowing vines, and the furniture had been rearranged in bizarre, gravity-defying formations. A couch floated upside-down near the ceiling, and the coffee table was perched precariously on one leg, spinning in slow circles.

"Well," Brie said, coughing, "that's one way to redecorate."

Lisa rubbed the back of her neck, looking sheepish. "Sorry, guys. I was trying to make an anti-gravity potion, but I think I overdid it."

"You think?" Charmina's voice cut through the murmurs of the crowd as she marched into the centre of the room, her expression as sharp as ever. "This is exactly the kind of reckless behaviour that will keep you here longer! And the rest of us too – if you don't admit to being the one behind this."

"Oh, relax," Melinda said. "It's not like anyone got hurt."

"That's not the point," Charmina snapped. "The headmistress will hear about this, and you know she doesn't take kindly to chaos."

Melinda rolled her eyes. "It's a magic school, Charmina. Chaos is kind of the point."

Charmina glared at her. "Some of us are trying to earn our way out of here, Melinda. Maybe you should try it sometime."

Melinda bristled, ready to retort, but before the argument could escalate, a loud chime echoed through the room. The glowing vines on the walls began to fade, and the furniture slowly returned to its rightful place.

"That's the gong," Melinda said, stretching. "Guess that's our cue to scatter before the staff show up."

Charmina muttered something under her breath and stalked out of the room, her entourage trailing behind her.

Lisa sighed, kicking at a stray shard of glass from the broken bottle. "Sorry, guys. I didn't mean to cause a scene."

"Don't stress about it," Melinda said, clapping her on the back. "It was entertaining. Besides, it's not like Charmina ever needs an excuse to lecture us."

Brie smirked. "Yeah, I bet she enjoyed it. I'm not going to say anything to anyone about this. I enjoyed the show."

Lisa managed a small smile. "Thanks, guys. I owe you one."

As the students began to disperse, Melinda turned to Brie. "So, what do you think? Still hate it here, or are we growing on you?"

Brie hesitated, glancing around the room. For all its weirdness – and the occasional dose of high drama – Ravenscroft was starting to feel... less awful.

"I'll let you know," she said, a small grin tugging at the corners of her mouth.

Chapter Five

The next morning, Brie woke up to find a piece of parchment slipped under her door. She groaned, dragging herself out of bed and squinting at the handwritten note:

All students report to the Great Hall immediately. Attendance is mandatory.
– Madam Delacroix

"Mandatory assemblies already?" she muttered, crumpling the paper in her hand. "This place really knows how to ruin a morning."

Melinda was waiting for her just down the hallway, looking equally unimpressed.

"Let me guess," Brie said, falling into step beside her. "The headmistress wants to lecture us about Lisa's potion mishap."

"Probably," Melinda said with a shrug. "Or maybe Charmina finally tattled her way into running the place."

The Great Hall was already packed when they arrived, the students buzzing in their seats with speculation. Madam Delacroix stood at the front, her imposing figure framed by two glowing sigils etched into the stone floor. She raised a hand, and the room fell silent.

"Students," she began, her voice carrying effortlessly across the hall, "as you are all aware, Ravenscroft is a place of discipline and rehabilitation. However, it is also a place of tradition. And one such tradition is upon us."

Brie exchanged a confused glance with Melinda.

"I am speaking, of course, about the Ravenscroft Ball," Madam Delacroix continued. "An opportunity for you to demonstrate your growth, your refinement, and your understanding of the values we uphold."

A murmur rippled through the crowd.

"A ball?" Brie whispered to Melinda. "Seriously?"

"Yep," Melinda said, smirking. "It's their way of pretending we're civilised."

The headmistress clapped her hands, and a burst of magical energy swept through the room. Small scrolls appeared in mid-air, one landing neatly in front of each student. Brie unrolled hers and scanned the contents:

Attendance mandatory. Formal attire required. Magical conduct to be evaluated.

"Great," Brie muttered. "A dress-up party with homework."

"Oh, don't be so grumpy," Melinda said, nudging her. "It's not all bad. Think of it as a chance to really annoy Charmina."

Brie laughed. "Now *that's* a tradition I can get behind."

***

The days leading up to the ball were a mix of chaos and grumbling as the students prepared. For some, it was an opportunity to show off their magical tailoring skills, crafting elaborate gowns and suits with spells that made the fabric shimmer or change colour. For Brie, it was just another headache.

"You know," Brie said, glaring at the fabric spread across her bed, "I think I grew out of playing dress-up a good few years ago now."

Melinda, sitting cross-legged on the floor with a needle and thread in hand, rolled her eyes. "Relax. It's not like they're expecting us to waltz around like we're at some royal court. Just throw something together and call it a day."

"Easy for you to say," Brie muttered. "You've probably had your outfit planned since last year."

"I'm more of a last-minute kind of girl. But you..." Melinda eyed Brie critically, her gaze lingering on her untamed green hair. "You've got a look. Might as well own it."

Brie sighed, flopping onto her bed. "Fine. What screams "witch who doesn't care about dumb traditions and would rather be doing something else"?"

"Green," Melinda said without hesitation.

Brie raised an eyebrow. "Green? Isn't that a little... on the nose?"

"Exactly," Melinda said, grinning. "Lean into it. Own the green."

Chapter Six

The night of the ball arrived faster than Brie expected. The Great Hall had been transformed into something almost unrecognisable. Chandeliers floated lower than usual, their golden light casting a warm glow over a wide dance floor and rows of chairs along the walls. Soft, haunting melodies came from the corner of the room. The instruments, enchanted to hover effortlessly, played themselves, filling the space with an ethereal yet distinctly rock-infused sound. An electric violin weaved a mournful tune, its notes lingering in the air, while a guitar hummed in deep, soulful chords. A bass thrummed beneath it all, and a set of drums, suspended in mid-air, provided a subtle rhythm.

Brie lingered near the entrance, tugging at the hem of her dress. It was a deep emerald ball gown, simple yet striking, and matched her hair almost perfectly. Melinda had insisted on helping her with her makeup, adding a hint of shimmer to her eyes that Brie had reluctantly admitted didn't look half bad.

"Looking sharp," Melinda said, sidling up beside her in a flowing black gown with silver accents.

"You're one to talk," Brie replied, giving her a once-over. "You clean up surprisingly well."

Melinda winked. "Don't get used to it."

The students were scattered across the grand hall in small, loosely formed clusters, chatting in hushed tones, laughing, and exchanging nervous glances as the evening stretched on. A few wandered aimlessly around the edges of the dance floor, unsure of where to position themselves. In the midst of it all, Charmina stood near the front, looking as poised and untouchable as ever. Her pristine white gown shimmered under the overhead lights, making her appear almost ethereal, like a character pulled straight from the pages of a fairy-tale book.

The perfection of her appearance was almost painstaking, from the smoothness of her carefully styled blonde hair to the flawless cut of her dress. It was as if she had rehearsed for this moment, each detail carefully orchestrated, demanding attention.

Brie couldn't help but roll her eyes. "Ugh," she muttered under her breath, watching Charmina with a mix of disdain and disbelief. "She just loves herself way too much, doesn't she?"

Grinning mischievously, Melinda leaned closer to Brie, her voice low but filled with a hint of excitement. "Let's take her down a peg, shall we?" Her tone was playful but also brimming with the kind of anticipation that suggested she had something in mind.

Before Brie could even think to ask what Melinda meant, Melinda's eyes gleamed with purpose. She raised her hand, her fingers curling slightly as if readying herself for a spell. There was a murmur of words under her breath, almost inaudible beneath the music. Brie strained to listen, but all she caught were a few indistinct syllables. Then, to her surprise, a faint shimmer of magic swirled around Melinda's fingers like a whisper of light, darting towards Charmina in a swift, barely noticeable motion.

Brie held her breath, her heart skipping a beat. For a moment, nothing changed. The room continued as it was, the students still milling about and chatting in small groups, unaware of the brewing mischief. But then, slowly, a small, almost imperceptible change began to take shape.

Charmina's flawless hair – so perfectly styled and immovable just moments before – began to shift. At first, it was subtle, barely noticeable, but Brie could see the strands at the top of Charmina's head lift, one by one, as though an invisible hand was tugging at them. As the moments passed, the effect became more pronounced, and Charmina's hair seemed to defy gravity, slowly rising up as though it had been caught in a fierce gust of wind. It was as if the invisible force had a mind of its own, tousling her meticulously arranged locks into a frizzy, uncontrollable mess.

Brie watched with wide eyes, a grin threatening to break free as she observed the unexpected scene unfolding before them. Charmina's perfectly composed expression began to falter. She reached up, hands flustered, to pat her hair down, as though trying to restore some semblance of control over it. But when she realised what was happening, her fingers froze mid-motion, as though she had come to the unsettling realisation that she couldn't stop the magic at work.

"You didn't?!" Brie said to Melinda.

"I did," Melinda said, her eyes twinkling with a blend of satisfaction and delight. She crossed her arms as if to say she had absolutely no regrets.

Charmina's piercing gaze locked onto Brie and Melinda with a sharpness that could cut through steel. It was clear that despite the number of students in attendance, she knew exactly where to look.

Brie swallowed, her smile faltering slightly as she exchanged a quick, knowing look with Melinda.

"You two!" Charmina seethed, marching towards them. "What did you do?"

"Us?" Brie said, feigning innocence. "We're just enjoying the party."

"Don't play dumb," Charmina snapped. "I know this is something to do with you."

Before Brie could respond, the headmistress' voice rang out over the crowd.

"Enough!"

The room, instruments included, fell silent as Madam Delacroix stepped forward, her sharp gaze sweeping over the students. She didn't need to raise her voice; her presence alone was enough to command attention.

"I trust we are all capable of behaving ourselves," she said, her tone icy. "This is supposed to be a sophisticated occasion, not a circus."

Brie felt her cheeks flush as the headmistress' gaze lingered on her and Melinda. She glanced at Melinda, who appeared unfazed, though there seemed to be the faintest hint of guilt tucked behind her smirk.

"Now," Madam Delacroix continued, her voice softening slightly, "let us enjoy the evening."

The instruments resumed playing, and the tension in the room began to dissipate. Charmina shot Brie one last glare before storming off, her hair still wild and static despite her efforts to smooth it down.

"Worth it," Melinda whispered, nudging Brie.

Brie couldn't help but laugh. "You're terrible."

"And yet, here you are," Melinda replied, grinning.

***

As the evening wore on, Brie began to feel more at ease. Despite the formal setting, the ball wasn't as insufferable as she'd imagined. The students gradually loosened up, some dancing awkwardly to the band, others chatting in small clusters.

Melinda had drifted off to stir up more chaos somewhere, leaving Brie to her own devices. She lingered near the refreshment table, nibbling on a strange glowing pastry that tasted like citrus and starlight.

"You look like you're having *such* a good time," a voice drawled behind her.

Brie turned to see Charmina, her arms crossed and her expression as sour as ever.

"Charmina," Brie said, flashing a saccharine smile. "What a surprise. Shouldn't you be off dazzling the headmistress with your perfection?"

Charmina's lips thinned. "I don't need to impress anyone. Unlike you, I understand what's at stake here."

Brie raised an eyebrow. "And what's that supposed to mean?"

"It means," Charmina said, stepping closer, "that while you and your little sidekick are busy playing pranks, the rest of us are actually trying to improve ourselves. Some of us have goals beyond making a mockery of this academy."

Brie's smile faltered, replaced by a sharp glare. "Newsflash, Charmina: not everyone wants to live their life as a walking rulebook. Maybe you should try loosening up for once."

"And maybe you should try taking something seriously," Charmina shot back.

The tension between them was thick enough to cut with a knife. Brie opened her mouth to retort, but before she could, the room shook with a sudden, violent tremor.

The chandeliers above swayed precariously, their lights flickering. Students stumbled, clutching onto tables and each other as the ground beneath them rumbled.

"What the hell?" Brie muttered, her earlier irritation forgotten.

A crackling sound filled the air, and a jagged tear appeared in the centre of the room. Magic pulsed from it in waves, dark and volatile, and the air around it seemed to ripple like heat off asphalt.

"Stay back!" Madam Delacroix's voice rang out, sharp and commanding.

The students scrambled to the edges of the hall as the headmistress stepped forward, her hands glowing with a faint, golden light.

"What is that?" Brie whispered to Melinda, who had reappeared at her side, her expression uncharacteristically serious.

"Looks like someone tampered with some wards," Melinda said, her voice low. "Badly."

Madam Delacroix raised her hands, chanting under her breath. The glow around her fingers intensified, spreading outward in a wave of golden light that pushed against the crackling tear. For a moment, it seemed to work – the rift began to shrink, its edges smoothing out.

But then the tear flared violently, sending a shockwave through the room that knocked Madam Delacroix back several steps.

"What's going on?" Charmina's voice was tight with panic as she joined them.

"Probably someone being stupid," Melinda said, though her tone lacked its usual flippancy. "Wards don't just break on their own."

Brie's gaze darted around the room, looking for clues. Her eyes landed on a group of students huddled near the far wall, their faces pale and anxious. One of them – Lisa – was clutching a small, glowing artefact that pulsed with the same chaotic energy as the rift.

"Oh, for the love of..." Brie groaned, marching towards them.

"Wait, Brie!" Melinda called after her, but Brie didn't stop.

She reached the group and grabbed Lisa by the arm. "What did you do?"

Lisa's eyes widened, her hands trembling as she held up the artefact. "I didn't mean to! I thought it was just a focus crystal! I didn't know it would..."

"Of course you didn't," Brie snapped, snatching the artefact from her hands. It thrummed with unstable energy, sending tingling sensations up her arm.

"Brie, don't..." Charmina began, but Brie ignored her.

"Everyone stand back!" Brie shouted, holding the artefact in front of her.

She wasn't entirely confident of what she was doing, but she wasn't about to let the entire room collapse because of someone else's screw-up. Taking a deep breath, she focused on the artefact, willing the frantic energy to subside.

It fought her at first, the magic lashing out like a cornered animal. But Brie refused to let go. She muttered under her breath, channelling what little control she had into the artefact, pushing back against the chaos.

Slowly, the energy began to stabilise. The rift in the centre of the room flickered, then closed with a sharp *snap*.

For a moment, there was silence. Then the students erupted into cheers and applause, their relief palpable.

Brie dropped the artefact onto the table with a clatter, her hands shaking.

"Well," she said, trying to catch her breath, "that wasn't so hard."

"Are you insane?" Charmina said through gritted teeth, grabbing her by the arm. "You could've got yourself killed!"

"Yeah, well," Brie said, pulling her arm free, "someone had to fix it, and you were too busy panicking."

Charmina's eyes narrowed, but she said nothing, turning on her heel and stalking away.

Melinda's expression was a blend of awe and concern. "That was... impressive. And stupid. Mostly stupid."

Brie smirked weakly. "What can I say? I like to keep things interesting."

***

By the time the dust had settled, the Great Hall looked worse for wear. Several chairs were overturned, the enchanted chandeliers flickered weakly, and faint scorch marks marred the floor where the rift had been. The headmistress stood in the centre of it all, her sharp gaze sweeping over the room like a hawk surveying its prey.

"Everyone is to return to their quarters immediately," she commanded, her voice cold. "This evening's events are over."

The students grumbled but obeyed, filing out of the hall in a wave of murmured conversations and nervous glances. Brie lingered near the edge of the room, avoiding the headmistress' gaze as she helped Melinda right an overturned chair.

"You think we're in trouble?" Brie whispered.

Melinda snorted. "Trouble is kind of our permanent state of existence, isn't it?"

Before Brie could reply, Madam Delacroix's voice cut through the air like a blade.

"Miss Holloway. Miss Sharpe."

Brie froze, exchanging a wary glance with Melinda.

They approached the headmistress cautiously, Brie bracing herself for the inevitable lecture.

"You both seem to have a penchant for chaos," the headmistress said, her tone measured but no less intimidating. "However, I must admit that tonight's events could have ended far worse without your intervention, Brie."

Brie blinked, caught off guard. "Wait, are you saying we're not in trouble?"

Madam Delacroix raised an eyebrow. "Do not mistake my acknowledgment for approval. The fact remains that someone tampered with a highly volatile artefact and endangered everyone in this room."

Her gaze shifted to Lisa, who was hovering near the exit, clearly trying to make herself invisible.

"You there," Madam Delacroix said, her voice cutting through the air like a whip.

Lisa flinched but reluctantly stepped forward. "Y-yes, Headmistress?"

"You will report to my office first thing tomorrow morning," Madam Delacroix said. "Do not make me summon you."

Lisa nodded quickly, her face pale. "Yes, Headmistress. I'm sorry."

Madam Delacroix's attention returned to Brie and Melinda. "As for you two, consider yourselves on probation. You may have prevented a disaster, Brie, but the pair of you have been at the centre of too many disturbances. Another incident, and I will not be so lenient."

"Yes, Headmistress," they said in unison, though Brie couldn't resist muttering under her breath, "Define lenient."

Madam Delacroix glared sharply at Brie, but instead of saying anything, she gestured for them to leave.

As they made their way back to the dormitories, Melinda let out a low whistle. "Well, that went better than expected."

"Barely," Brie said. "I swear that woman could freeze water just by looking at it."

"You've got to admit, though," Melinda said, her grin returning, "you kind of saved the day back there."

Brie rolled her eyes. "Yeah, because Lisa was about to turn the place into a crater."

"Still counts," Melinda said. "You're practically a hero."

"Please don't ever call me that again," Brie said, but she couldn't hide the small smile tugging at her lips.

Chapter Seven

A few days after the ball and its chaotic aftermath, life at Ravenscroft settled back into its usual rhythm – or as close to "usual" as a reform academy for rebellious witches could get. Brie had started to fall into a routine, albeit reluctantly: boring classes in the morning, mildly chaotic ones in the afternoon, and evenings spent in the common room where Melinda's schemes provided endless entertainment.

But as much as Brie hated to admit it, the cracks in her rebellious exterior were beginning to show. She found herself paying more attention in classes – especially Spellcraft – and even volunteered to demonstrate a minor charm in Magical Applications, shocking both the professor and her classmates.

"Who are you, and what have you done with Brie?" Melinda teased as they walked back to the dorms after class.

"Relax," Brie said, amused. "It's not like I'm becoming one of them."

Melinda raised an eyebrow. "Uh-huh. Sure you're not secretly trying to impress the headmistress?"

Brie rolled her eyes. "Please. If Madam Delacroix ever smiled, I think the universe would implode."

Still, Brie couldn't shake the feeling that something was shifting – not just within herself, but in the academy as a whole. The incident at the ball had left a strange energy lingering in the air, and while no one openly talked about it, Brie could tell she wasn't the only one who noticed.

One particularly dreary afternoon, Brie and Melinda found themselves assigned to the potion labs for a group project. The room was filled with the clinking of glassware and the soft bubbling of cauldrons as students worked in pairs to brew a basic binding potion. "Basic", of course, was a relative term at Ravenscroft.

"So, we just add the powdered roots and stir counter-clockwise?" Brie asked, frowning at the instructions.

"Counter-clockwise," Melinda confirmed. "And don't forget to chant the binding phrase, or it'll turn into glue."

Brie sighed, sprinkling the roots into the bubbling mixture and muttering the incantation under her breath. The potion turned a murky shade of green, emitting a faint shimmer that she hoped was a good sign.

"Not bad," Melinda said, peering into the cauldron. "You might actually have a knack for this."

"Don't jinx it," Brie said, but she couldn't help feeling a small sense of satisfaction.

Across the room, a familiar voice cut through the hum of activity.

"No, no, no! That's completely wrong!"

Brie turned to see Charmina standing over one of her classmates, her expression exasperated as she snatched a vial of powdered scales from their hands. "If you use too much of this, you'll destabilise the entire potion."

"Wow," Brie said to Melinda. "Charmina's really taking her role as the queen of potions seriously."

Melinda snickered. "I bet she dreams about correcting people in her sleep."

Unfortunately, Charmina overheard them. She straightened, fixing Brie with an icy glare. "At least I take my studies seriously," she said, her tone sharp. "Unlike some people."

Brie raised an eyebrow. "Some people still managed to save your perfect little evening at the ball, remember?"

Charmina's jaw tightened, but she didn't respond. Instead, she turned back to her partner, muttering something under her breath.

"Don't let her get to you," Melinda said, nudging Brie. "She's just mad because you're proving you're better at magic than she is."

Brie laughed. "Now that's a scary thought."

***

Later that night, just as Brie was starting to doze off, a faint knock at her door jolted her awake. Groaning, she threw off the duvet and shuffled to answer it.

When she opened the door, she was surprised to find Lisa standing there, her face pale and her hands fidgeting nervously.

"Lisa?" Brie said, frowning. "What are you doing here?"

"I need your help," Lisa whispered, glancing over her shoulder as though she was being followed.

Brie stepped aside, letting her in. "What's going on?"

Lisa hesitated, wringing her hands. "I... I think someone's messing with the wards again. I overheard some students talking in the library earlier, and they mentioned something about another artefact."

Brie's stomach sank. "You're kidding me. After what happened at the ball?"

Lisa shook her head, her red hair fanning around her face. "I don't know who's doing it, but... I don't know. I just have a bad feeling."

Brie ran a hand through her hair, trying to process the information. "Why come to me? Shouldn't you tell the headmistress or something?"

Lisa hesitated. "I thought about it, but... after what happened at the ball, I don't think she'll take me seriously. Besides, I don't want to be like Charmina."

Brie sighed, her mind racing. After what happened at the ball, she didn't want to get in way over her head. Although she had managed to stop the chaos before it got out of hand, she couldn't ignore the fact that the magic had been beyond her experience. She didn't feel fully capable of taking responsibility for something like that again.

Despite this, a part of her couldn't ignore the nervous energy in Lisa's voice.

"Fine," Brie said, grabbing her robe. "But if this turns out to be something bad – or if you've got the wrong end of the stick – you owe me a week's worth of snacks from the dining hall."

Lisa managed a weak smile. "Deal."

Chapter Eight

The academy was eerily silent as Brie and Lisa made their way through the dimly lit corridors. The faint glow of enchanted sconces cast long shadows on the stone walls, making the place feel more like a haunted mausoleum than a school.

"I guess they're still in the library?" Brie whispered, glancing over her shoulder to make sure they weren't being followed.

"I think so," Lisa replied, clutching her robes tightly around herself. "They were sitting in the back corner, whispering. I didn't recognise their voices, but they definitely mentioned an artefact."

"And you're sure they weren't just talking about homework?" Brie asked sceptically.

Lisa shot her a nervous look. "Pretty sure."

Brie sighed, adjusting her pace to keep Lisa from falling too far behind. "Alright. If they're still there, we'll confront them. If not, we go back to bed, and you start stockpiling snacks for me tomorrow."

The library was dark when they arrived, the doors creaking softly as Brie pushed them open. The only light came from the moonlight streaming through the tall, arched windows, casting silvery beams across the rows of bookshelves.

Lisa hesitated at the threshold, her eyes wide. "You're really going to go straight up to them?" she whispered. "Are you sure about this?"

"Nope," Brie said, stepping inside. "But we're here now, so let's make it count."

The pair moved cautiously through the aisles, their footsteps muffled by the thick carpet. Brie kept her ears sharp, straining to catch any hint of movement.

At first, there was nothing but the faint rustle of pages from the enchanted books that occasionally rearranged themselves on the shelves. But as they neared the back corner of the library, Brie's ears picked up faint voices – low, hurried whispers that carried just enough to be heard.

She held up a hand, motioning for Lisa to stop.

"...has to be tonight," one voice said, sharp and impatient.

"Are you crazy?" another replied, softer but no less urgent. "The wards are still unstable after the ball. If we get caught..."

"We won't get caught," the first voice snapped. "Now shut up and focus."

Brie inched closer, peering around the edge of a bookshelf. Two figures were crouched on the floor, their faces obscured by the hoods of their robes. Between them lay a small artefact, its surface glowing faintly with a sickly green light. Brie grimaced. It looked suspiciously similar to the one that had caused the rift at the ball.

"What now?" Lisa whispered, her voice trembling.

Brie thought for a moment. She could try to grab the artefact and run, but if the figures were as reckless as they sounded, that could backfire spectacularly. Instead, she decided on a different approach.

"Hey!" she called, stepping into view.

The figures froze, their heads snapping towards her in alarm. Brie caught glimpses of their features. One had a square jaw and a strong nose, his dark hair barely visible beneath his hood. The other had more delicate features with a softer jawline, though his sharp eyes were piercing through the dim light. His light brown hair, tangled and unkempt, peeked out from beneath his hood. Though she couldn't immediately recall their names, Brie had seen them in passing before; they were the type to keep to themselves, often blending into the crowd.

"Yeah, I'm talking to you," Brie said, crossing her arms. "What's going on?"

The dark-haired student scrambled to his feet, raising his hands defensively. "W-we're not doing anything!" he stammered.

"Uh-huh," Brie said, eyeing the glowing artefact. "Because that looks like nothing."

The other student remained on the floor. He grabbed the artefact, clutching it protectively. "Leave us alone!" he whispered aggressively. "You don't understand what's at stake!"

"Then explain it to me," Brie said, stepping closer.

The student on his feet hesitated, glancing at his companion. "We're trying to fix the wards," he said finally. "After the ball, we realised how vulnerable the academy is. If someone – or something – really wanted to, they could breach it again."

"And you think messing around with unstable artefacts is the solution?" Brie asked, raising an eyebrow. "Because last time Lisa tried doing that, it didn't go well!"

Lisa shuffled nervously, squirming with embarrassment at the truth of Brie's words. She shifted her weight from one foot to the other, but there was a quiet agreement in her stance, as if she knew Brie had a point.

"It's the only way!" the student on the floor insisted. "I'm not getting the professors involved with this. I've already broken several rules just to get my hands on this artefact. I don't want to end up stuck here longer than I have to be. We've got to sort this out by ourselves; now that we've started to tamper with this thing, we can't just leave it to its own devices. The magic – it could spiral out of control, and I can't risk letting it consume me, or worse. What if..."

"Ok, wait a moment," Brie interrupted, holding up a hand. "I get what you're saying, but this is way beyond you now. You need to hand that thing over to one of the professors before you make things worse."

Brie sighed inwardly, feeling a pang of discomfort. She was starting to sound like Charmina, but as much as she hated to admit it, this looked like something no student could handle on their own. The magic was volatile, too unpredictable – and potentially, harmful.

The student on the floor shook his head. "No. You don't understand..."

Before he could finish, the artefact began to pulse erratically, its glow intensifying.

"Oh, great," Brie muttered. "Lisa, stay behind me."

Lisa didn't need to be told twice.

The artefact's energy flared, sending out a wave of heat that rattled the nearby bookshelves. The student scrambled away from it and jumped to his feet, backing up as it began to crackle and spark.

Brie acted on instinct, muttering a quick spell under her breath. A shimmering barrier appeared between her and the artefact just as it released a burst of raw magic. The blast struck the barrier, dissipating harmlessly, but the force of it caused the ground to shudder beneath their feet, sending a wave of instability through the room. Brie, Lisa, and the two male students were thrown off balance. Each of them quickly grabbed onto the nearby bookshelves, their fingers gripping the wood tightly to steady themselves as the shelves rattled and creaked under the pressure.

"Still think you've got this under control?" Brie asked, glaring at the darker-haired guy.

He pulled back his hood, and as it fell away, his eyes became more apparent – wide and fearful, filled with panic. "We didn't mean for this to happen…"

"Yeah, well, that's what happens when you play with things you don't understand," Brie snapped.

She knelt, carefully picking up the artefact, her fingers brushing its cool surface. The glow had dimmed, but it still emitted a faint hum, an unsettling vibration that thrummed in her hands. Small but intricate, it was shaped like a twisted, jagged crystal, its edges sharp and uneven. Dark veins of some unknown substance pulsed beneath its surface, hinting at the volatile magic contained within. Despite its size, it felt heavier than it looked, as if holding the weight of something ancient and dangerous.

"We're taking this to Madam Delacroix," Brie said firmly. "And if you try to stop us, I'll make sure she knows exactly who to blame."

Brie couldn't help but cringe inwardly. She sounded so much like Charmina. It unsettled her, the idea that she was slipping into the very same role she'd so quickly grown to dislike. But this situation was different. She could feel the pulsing energy of the artefact in her hands, its raw power still unpredictable.

"This isn't something we can handle on our own," she muttered to herself, trying to push the uncomfortable feeling away. "We need someone who knows what they're doing."

Lisa remained silent, her eyes flicking to the artefact with obvious trepidation, but Brie could see she agreed. There was no other choice. They needed an expert – someone who could stop the chaos that had been activated before it spiralled out of control.

"Fine," said the other guy, his hood still up. "Just... be careful with it."

Brie rolled her eyes. With a firm grip on the artefact, she motioned for Lisa to follow her. "Come on," she said. "Let's get this over with."

Brie and Lisa made their way towards the headmistress' office, the artefact's faint hum impossible to ignore as they walked. The corridors felt darker than usual, the flickering sconces casting ominous shadows that seemed to stretch and twist as they passed.

"I bet we'll get blamed for this whole thing now," Lisa said quietly, her voice trembling.

"Great," Brie muttered. "That's real comforting."

When they finally reached the tall, imposing doors of Madam Delacroix's office, Brie hesitated. It wasn't that she was afraid of the headmistress – ok, maybe a little – but the idea of explaining this whole mess wasn't exactly appealing.

"You knock," Brie said, glancing at Lisa.

"What? No way," Lisa said, taking a step back. "This was your idea."

Brie sighed, rolling her eyes. "Fine. Coward." She rapped on the door three times, the sound echoing through the corridor.

"Enter," came Madam Delacroix's sharp voice from within.

Brie pushed the door open, stepping inside with Lisa close behind. The office was as intimidating as ever, with its dark wood panelling, towering bookshelves, and the ever-present hum of magic in the air. Madam Delacroix sat behind her massive desk, her piercing gaze locked onto the two of them.

"Miss Holloway," she said, her tone clipped. "Miss Lockwood. To what do I owe this... late-night visit?"

Brie placed the artefact carefully on the edge of the desk. "We found this in the library," she said, keeping her tone as neutral as possible. "Some students were messing with it, and things got... a bit too serious."

Madam Delacroix's eyes narrowed as she examined the artefact. "And who, precisely, were these students?"

Brie and Lisa exchanged a quick glance, a silent agreement passing between them. Neither of them spoke. The hesitation hung heavy in the air.

Madam Delacroix's sharp eyes flicked between them, her lips pressing into a thin line. "Very well," she said after a moment, her tone cool but knowing.

The headmistress reached out, her hand hovering over the artefact as though testing its energy. The artefact sparked faintly.

"This is a dangerous relic," she said, her voice low.

"Yeah, we kind of figured that out the hard way," Brie said.

Madam Delacroix shot her a sharp look, and Brie quickly shut her mouth.

"You were right to bring this to me," Madam Delacroix said, her tone begrudgingly approving. "Although I am curious how you came to be involved in this matter."

"Lisa overheard someone talking," Brie said. "She told me, and we went to check it out. Good thing we did – otherwise, the library might have turned into a crater by now."

Madam Delacroix's expression softened ever so slightly as she turned to Lisa. "That was brave of you, Miss Lockwood. Foolish, perhaps, but brave."

Lisa flushed, ducking her head. "Thank you, Headmistress."

"As for you, Miss Holloway..." Madam Delacroix's gaze returned to Brie, and Brie braced herself for another lecture. But instead, the headmistress' tone was measured, almost contemplative. "You continue to surprise me. I had you pegged as a troublemaker with no regard for the rules. Yet here you are, taking responsibility for a situation that could have ended in disaster."

Brie blinked, caught off guard. "Uh... thanks?"

"Do not mistake my words for praise," Madam Delacroix said quickly, though there was a faint glimmer of something in her eyes – approval, maybe? "This does not absolve you of your past infractions. But it does suggest that there may be more to you than meets the eye."

Brie smirked. "I'll take that as a compliment."

Madam Delacroix sighed, pinching the bridge of her nose. "Both of you are dismissed. Return to your quarters, and I will handle the rest."

"Yes, Headmistress," Brie and Lisa said in unison.

As they left the office, Brie let out a long breath she hadn't realised she'd been holding.

"Well," she said, glancing at Lisa, "that wasn't as bad as I thought it'd be."

Lisa managed a small smile. "Thanks, by the way. For helping me."

Brie waved her off. "Don't mention it. Just be glad you don't owe me any snacks."

Lisa laughed softly as they parted ways, heading to their respective rooms.

As Brie settled into bed, she found herself replaying the events of the night in her mind. It felt good to have done something worthwhile.

"Maybe I'm not so bad at this after all," she muttered, pulling the covers over her head.

She drifted off to sleep with the faintest hint of a smile on her lips, already wondering what tomorrow would bring.

Chapter Nine

The next morning, Brie woke to a knock at her door. She groaned, rubbing her eyes as she sat up.

"It's me," Melinda's voice called from the other side.

Brie sighed and shuffled to the door, opening it to find Melinda holding a steaming cup of what might pass for coffee.

"Morning, sunshine," Melinda said, grinning as she handed over the cup.

"Why are you so chipper?" Brie muttered, taking a sip.

"Because," Melinda said, plopping onto Brie's bed, "word on the grapevine is that you saved the library from becoming a magical crater last night."

Brie frowned. "How does everyone know about that already?"

"Welcome to Ravenscroft," Melinda said with a shrug. "Secrets don't last here. Besides, Lisa's been talking."

Brie groaned. "Great. Just what I need – my heroics being blown out of proportion."

"Relax," Melinda said, smirking. "You're not getting a medal or anything. Though you *did* earn a little street cred with the other students. Even Charmina's been unusually quiet this morning."

Brie arched an eyebrow. "Charmina? Quiet? Are we talking about the same person?"

"I know, right?" Melinda said. "It's like she doesn't know how to handle you being the centre of attention for once."

Brie rolled her eyes, but a small part of her couldn't deny the satisfaction of having thrown Charmina off her game.

***

The rest of the day passed in a blur of classes and whispers. Everywhere Brie went, she caught snippets of conversations about the library incident. Some students looked at her with newfound respect, while others – like Charmina – seemed irritated by her sudden popularity.

By the time evening rolled around, Brie was more than ready for some peace and quiet. She headed to the common room, hoping to unwind with a book or maybe just enjoy Melinda's antics from a safe distance.

Instead, she found herself greeted by an unexpected sight.

A group of students had gathered near the fireplace, their attention focused on Charmina, who was holding court like a queen addressing her subjects.

"This is exactly what I've been saying all along," Charmina said, her voice loud enough to carry across the room as she flicked her blonde hair with an air of importance. "Although it's brave to intervene, the risk is too high. If it goes wrong, we could all be held responsible. I know I'm not the only one here with aspirations to go home one day. Do we really want the actions of others – no matter how brave they might seem – ruining that chance for the rest of us?"

Brie snorted. "What's her deal now?"

Melinda rolled her eyes. "Apparently, she's on some crusade to "restore order". Typical Charmina."

Brie leaned against the wall, watching as Charmina continued her speech. Most of the students looked bored, but a few nodded along, clearly buying into her rhetoric.

"Of course," Charmina added, her gaze flicking towards Brie, "some people don't seem to care about putting everyone else at risk."

Brie straightened, her temper flaring. "Excuse me?"

The room fell silent as all eyes turned to her. Charmina smirked, clearly pleased to have baited her.

"I'm just saying," Charmina said, her tone saccharine, "that some of us would like to go home and not have our chances jeopardised by students who want to play at being a hero."

Brie pushed off the wall, crossing the room to stand in front of Charmina. "You've got a lot of nerve, considering you weren't anywhere near the library when things went sideways last night."

"I follow the rules," Charmina said, her voice cold. "Unlike you."

"And yet I'm the one who stopped that artefact from blowing up the entire library," Brie shot back. "What were you doing? Practicing your perfect posture?"

A few students snickered, and Charmina's cheeks flushed.

"Enough!"

The sharp voice of the headmistress cut through the tension like a knife. She stood in the doorway, her expression as stern as ever.

"Miss Lovelace," Madam Delacroix said, her gaze pinning Charmina in place. "I appreciate your enthusiasm for maintaining order, but stirring up division among your peers is not the way to do it."

Charmina opened her mouth to protest, but the headmistress raised a hand, silencing her.

"And Miss Holloway," Madam Delacroix continued, turning her attention to Brie, "while your actions in the library were commendable, I suggest you focus on leading by example rather than engaging in petty arguments."

Brie bit back a retort, nodding reluctantly. "Yes, Headmistress."

Madam Delacroix's gaze swept over the rest of the room. "I expect better from all of you. This academy is not a playground for egos or grudges. If you want to prove yourselves, do so through your actions."

With that, she turned and swept out of the room, leaving an uncomfortable silence in her wake.

Brie glanced at Charmina, whose expression was a blend of anger and embarrassment.

For once, Brie decided not to push further. She turned and walked back to Melinda, muttering, "Well, that was fun."

Melinda grinned. "You've got a real talent for getting under Charmina's skin, you know that?"

"Yeah," Brie said, smiling, albeit a little uncomfortably. "But I think I'll take a break from that for now."

Chapter Ten

T he following week brought a mix of relief and monotony as the unrest surrounding the library incident began to fade. Classes resumed their usual dull pace, and the students settled back into their routines. Even Charmina seemed to back off, though Brie could tell from the occasional glare that the truce was tenuous at best.

Brie had just started to enjoy the relative calm when an announcement from the headmistress threw everything into upheaval again.

"Attention, students," Madam Delacroix's voice echoed through the hallways, carried by a magical amplification spell. "There will be a mandatory assessment this weekend. Details will be provided during tomorrow's morning assembly. Attendance is not optional."

Brie groaned, leaning her head against her desk. "An assessment? What does that even mean?"

"Knowing Madam Delacroix, it probably involves something dangerous and unnecessarily dramatic," Melinda said.

"Fantastic," Brie muttered. "Just when things were starting to feel normal."

"Normal is overrated," Melinda said with a grin. "Besides, it could be fun. You know, if you don't like having the weekend to relax."

"Ha!" Brie said dryly.

The next morning, the Great Hall was abuzz with speculation as students gathered for the assembly. Brie and Melinda found seats near the back, where they could keep a low profile – or so they hoped.

Madam Delacroix appeared at the front of the room, her robes billowing as she strode to the podium. The room fell silent almost instantly, the weight of her presence demanding attention.

"As many of you know," she began, "Ravenscroft is not merely a place of discipline. It is also a place of growth. Your time here is meant to prepare you not only as witches who can navigate society, but as individuals who can contribute something positive."

Brie exchanged a sceptical look with Melinda, who rolled her eyes.

"Therefore," Madam Delacroix continued, "we will be conducting an assessment to evaluate your progress. This will be a practical exercise, designed to test your abilities, your resourcefulness, and your capacity to work as a team."

"Teamwork?" Melinda whispered. "That's a new one."

"Each group will be assigned a challenge," Madam Delacroix said, her gaze sweeping over the room. "The details will remain undisclosed until the assessment begins. Suffice it to say, success will require co-operation and ingenuity."

Brie groaned softly. "Great. Group work. My favourite."

Melinda smirked. "Relax. Maybe you'll get lucky and end up with me."

Brie snorted. "Or I'll get stuck with Charmina. That's my luck."

When the group assignments were posted later that day, Brie's worst fears were confirmed.

"No," she said, staring at the parchment on the wall. "This has to be a joke."

"Looks like fate hates you as much as Charmina does," Melinda said, trying – and failing – not to laugh.

Brie's name was listed alongside Charmina's, as well as two other students she barely knew: a quiet girl named Thea and a lanky guy named Marcus who always seemed on the verge of falling asleep.

"This is going to be a disaster," Brie muttered, running a hand through her green hair.

"Hey, maybe it won't be so bad," Melinda said, patting her on the shoulder. "Charmina might surprise you."

Brie shot her a look. "Do you even believe that?"

"Not for a second," Melinda said, grinning.

***

The day of the assessment arrived, and the students gathered in the courtyard, bundled against the morning chill. The sky was overcast, coating everything in muted grey tones, and the air buzzed with nervous energy.

Brie stood with her assigned group, trying to avoid eye contact with Charmina, who was already giving instructions.

"Ok, here's the plan," Charmina said, her voice brisk. "We'll focus on efficiency and avoid unnecessary risks. That means no improvisation, no shortcuts, and no reckless behaviour."

Brie crossed her arms. "You mean no fun."

"This isn't about fun," Charmina snapped. "It's about passing."

"Whatever you say, Captain Perfect," Brie muttered.

Thea and Marcus exchanged wary glances but said nothing.

Before the argument could escalate, Madam Delacroix's voice rang out across the courtyard.

"Your challenges will begin shortly," she announced. "Remember, success depends on your ability to work together. Good luck."

With a wave of her hand, a series of glowing portals appeared, each marked with a group number. Brie sighed as she spotted their portal, the swirling energy radiating an ominous hum.

"Here we go," she muttered, stepping through.

The portal deposited them in a dense; foggy forest, the air thick with the scent of damp earth and moss. The only sounds were the faint rustle of leaves and the occasional distant birdcall.

A parchment materialised in front of Charmina, who snatched it up and read it aloud.

"Your challenge: locate the enchanted artefact hidden within the forest and return it to the portal. Be warned: obstacles lie in your path."

"Vague much?" Brie said, peering into the mist.

Charmina ignored her, folding the parchment neatly and tucking it into her robe. "Alright, let's move quickly and stay together. The sooner we find the artefact, the better."

"And if we run into obstacles?" Brie asked, smirking.

"We handle them without unnecessary risks," Charmina said firmly.

Brie rolled her eyes but followed as the group began to move deeper into the forest. The trees seemed to close in around them, their gnarled branches forming eerie shapes in the fog.

"Anyone else getting haunted-woods vibes?" Marcus muttered, his usual lethargy replaced by unease.

"Just keep moving," Charmina said. "We'll be fine as long as we stay focused."

Brie couldn't help but feel a twinge of doubt. Something about the forest felt wrong, as if it was alive and watching them. The deeper they ventured, the thicker the fog became. It swirled around their ankles, rising in patches that made it hard to see more than a few feet ahead. Branches twisted and creaked, leaves rustled with no breeze, and the distant sound of something skittering in the underbrush kept everyone on edge.

"This is ridiculous," Brie said, stepping over a moss-covered root. "How are we supposed to find an artefact in all this?"

"We'll find it faster if you stop complaining and start looking," Charmina said sharply, her eyes scanning the trees.

Brie opened her mouth to retort but stopped when she heard Marcus whisper, "Uh, guys? What's that?"

They all turned to where he was pointing. In the distance, a faint, pulsing glow pierced through the fog, its green light flickering like a heartbeat.

"That has to be it," Charmina said, her tone decisive. "Come on."

As they moved towards the light, Brie's feeling of unease grew more intense. The air seemed heavier, and the ground beneath their feet turned from soft moss to hard, cracked earth.

"This feels too easy," Brie muttered, glancing at Thea, who nodded nervously.

"It's not easy," Charmina snapped. "It's just straightforward. Stay focused."

But as they reached the source of the light, Brie's instincts proved correct.

The artefact – a jagged crystal the size of a fist – hovered a few feet off the ground, its glow casting eerie shadows across the clearing. Surrounding it were five massive stone statues, each resembling an unnaturally large, broad-shouldered man, but with monstrous, beast-like features. Their snarling faces were frozen in mid-roar, their heavy limbs and exaggerated proportions giving them an unsettling, almost living presence.

"Let me guess," Brie said, eyeing the statues warily. "They come to life if we touch the crystal."

Charmina huffed. "Not necessarily. Let's just think this through."

Thea, who had been silent for most of the journey, stepped closer, her voice hesitant. "The parchment said there would be obstacles. Maybe we have to confront them somehow?"

"Great," Brie said. "And how do we confront killer statues?"

"Carefully," Charmina said, her tone clipped. "I'll retrieve the artefact. The rest of you stay alert in case anything happens."

Brie rolled her eyes.

Charmina stepped forward, her movements slow and deliberate. The moment her fingers brushed the artefact, the statues sprang to life. Their stone limbs cracked and groaned as they moved, their glowing red eyes locking onto the group.

"Called it," Brie muttered.

"Run!" Charmina shouted, clutching the artefact as she bolted towards the group.

The statues roared, their heavy footsteps shaking the ground as they gave chase. Brie fired a quick spell at the nearest one, but the blast barely left a scorch mark on its stone surface.

"Ok, bad idea," she said, ducking as one of the statues swung a massive arm in her direction.

"What do we do?" Thea cried, her voice high-pitched with panic.

"Scatter!" Charmina yelled.

The group split, dodging through the trees as the statues lumbered after them. Brie darted to the left, narrowly avoiding a crushing blow from one of the stone behemoths.

"This is insane!" she shouted, firing another spell that ricocheted harmlessly off a statue's chest.

"You think?" Marcus called from somewhere to her right.

Brie skidded to a halt behind a fallen log, her mind racing. Spells didn't work, and the statues were too strong to fight head-on. But maybe...

"Guys!" she shouted. "We need to outsmart them! Lure them away from the clearing!"

"What about the artefact?" Charmina called back, her voice strained.

"Just keep it safe!" Brie said. "I've got an idea!"

She climbed onto the log, waving her arms to get the attention of one of the statues. "Hey, rock-for-brains! Over here!"

The statue turned towards her with a roar, its heavy steps shaking the ground as it charged. Brie leapt off the log and ran, weaving through the trees as the statue pursued her.

She led it into a dense thicket, where the trees grew close together, their twisted branches forming a natural barrier. The statue followed, but its massive size made it slow and clumsy in the confined space.

"Come on," Brie muttered, glancing over her shoulder. "Just a little further..."

The statue tried to force its way through the thicket, but its arm caught on a low branch. The branch snapped back like a spring, slamming into the statue's face and knocking it off balance. With a loud crash, the statue toppled, its limbs tangled in the dense undergrowth.

"Yes!" Brie shouted, punching the air.

She turned to head back to the clearing, but before she could move, another statue emerged from the fog, its glowing eyes locked onto her.

"Oh, come on!" she groaned.

The statue charged, and Brie raised her hand, firing a spell at its feet. The ground beneath the statue cracked, and it stumbled, giving her just enough time to dive out of the way.

"Brie!"

She looked up to see Charmina and the others running towards her, the artefact clutched tightly in Charmina's hand.

As Brie dodged another swing from the statue closest to her, the group backed into a tight circle, the remaining statues closing in around them. Brie's mind raced, searching for a solution.

"Wait," she said suddenly, her eyes narrowing. "The artefact – it's powering them, isn't it?"

Charmina hesitated, then nodded. "It has to be."

"Then we need to overload it," Brie said. "If we hit it with enough magic, it might disrupt the connection."

"That could destroy it," Charmina said.

"Do you have a better idea?" Brie snapped.

Charmina frowned but didn't argue. She held the artefact out, and Brie raised her hand, her energy focusing on a single point.

"Everyone, aim for the crystal!" Brie shouted.

Thea and Marcus joined in, their spells combining with Brie's and Charmina's in a surge of energy. The artefact began to glow brighter and brighter, its surface cracking under the strain.

With a deafening *boom*, the artefact shattered, sending a wave of energy rippling through the forest. The statues froze mid-step, their glowing eyes flickering out before they crumbled to the ground in heaps of stone.

For a moment, there was only silence. Then Charmina let out a long breath, clutching her knees as she bent over. "That... was reckless."

Brie grinned, her chest heaving. "Maybe, but it worked."

Chapter Eleven

The forest seemed eerily quiet now. The faint hum of the shattered artefact's energy had faded into nothingness, leaving only the rustle of leaves and the distant cawing of a crow. Brie leaned against a nearby tree, catching her breath as the adrenaline ebbed from her veins.

"Well," she said, brushing her hair out of her face, "that wasn't so bad."

Charmina straightened, fixing Brie with a sharp glare. "Not so bad? You destroyed the artefact! That might be counted as a fail."

Brie shrugged, pushing off the tree. "I'm pretty sure getting flattened by stone giants would've been worse."

"She's got a point," Marcus chimed in.

Charmina threw her hands up in exasperation. "You can't just..."

"Guys," Thea interrupted, her voice soft but urgent. "We need to get back to the portal. The assessment isn't over yet."

Brie nodded. "Thea's right. Let's move before something else decides to wake up."

***

The group emerged in the courtyard, where the other students were already gathering. Some looked exhausted, others exhilarated, but all of them wore expressions of relief to be back on familiar ground.

Madam Delacroix stood at the front of the crowd, her sharp gaze sweeping over the students as they assembled.

"Congratulations," she said, her voice carrying effortlessly across the courtyard. "You have all completed the assessment. The purpose of this exercise was to challenge you, to push you beyond your limits and force you to rely on one another. While the results were mixed, I am pleased to see that most of you rose to the occasion. Take the remainder of the day to reflect on your experiences. Classes will resume tomorrow."

With that, the crowd began to disperse, students chatting excitedly about their challenges.

Brie turned to Thea and Marcus, giving them a nod. "Nice work out there."

"You too," Thea said, smiling.

"Yeah," Marcus added. "For what it's worth, I'm glad you were on our team. Even if Charmina isn't."

Brie laughed. "Thanks. Let's just hope she doesn't try to strangle me in class tomorrow."

***

Later that evening, Brie found herself back in the common room, sprawled on one of the couches with Melinda beside her.

"So," Melinda said, tossing a small bag of snacks onto Brie's lap, "word is you took out a bunch of killer statues and destroyed an artefact."

Brie smirked, tearing open the bag. "I had a good team."

Melinda snorted. "Even with Charmina? Really? I need details."

Brie launched into a dramatic retelling of the challenge. Just as she was getting to the part about how she narrowly missed being hit by several pounds of stone, the door to the common room creaked open, and Charmina stepped inside, her expression unreadable. Brie tensed, half expecting a confrontation.

"I need to talk to you," Charmina said to Brie, her tone oddly calm.

Melinda raised an eyebrow. "Should I leave?"

"No," Charmina said, shaking her head. "This won't take long."

Brie sat up, crossing her arms. "Alright. What's on your mind?"

Charmina hesitated, glancing at Melinda before meeting Brie's gaze. "I just wanted to say thank you. For stepping up during the challenge."

Brie blinked, caught off guard. "Uh... you're welcome?"

"You may not care about the rules," Charmina said, her voice softer than usual, "but you care about people. And that's... something."

Before Brie could respond, Charmina turned and left.

Melinda whistled. "Wow. Did Charmina just..."

"Yeah," Brie said, still staring at the door. "Weird, right?"

Melinda grinned. "Looks like you've made a new friend."

"Let's not get carried away," Brie said, amused, and a little embarrassed.

As she settled back into the couch, a small part of her couldn't help but feel a strange sense of accomplishment.

Chapter Twelve

T he following day, Brie woke with a renewed sense of purpose. For the first time since arriving at Ravenscroft, she didn't feel entirely like an outsider. There was a small, nagging thought in the back of her mind: maybe this place wasn't so bad.

She threw on her robes and headed to breakfast, where Melinda was already waiting for her. The dining hall buzzed with chatter as students recounted their assessments, boasting about close calls and near victories.

"Morning, hero," Melinda said, grinning as Brie sat down. "What's on the agenda for today? Saving another library? Toppling another artefact?"

Brie smiled, grabbing a piece of toast. "I'm thinking I'll keep a low profile for once.

Besides, you haven't told me about your assessment yet."

Melinda shrugged. "Oh, you know, there's not much to tell really. We spotted the artefact pretty early on but figured it was way too obvious. Thought the whole thing was probably a trick – no way were we about to get lured into a pit of writhing shadow-vines or chased by some enchanted suits of armour for making the wrong move. So, we left the artefact where it was and focused on getting out. We didn't even touch it. Turns out, we were right. Lisa's group only had to touch their artefact for it to explode into a cloud of illusion magic. They got stuck in a looping maze for the rest of the test."

"So what? You all came back through the portal empty-handed?"

"Pretty much," Melinda said, not seeming too bothered by the whole thing.

Brie huffed a quiet laugh, shaking her head. "I didn't realise everyone had such a different experience."

"Yeah," Melinda said, seeming impressed. "Apparently, yours was the only group who managed to confront the artefact, even if you didn't come back with it."

Brie blinked, momentarily caught off guard. She hadn't really thought about how her group's performance stacked up against the others – she'd been too busy just trying to survive. But hearing it laid out like that was surprising.

They had charged in without hesitation, fought off enchanted statues, and ultimately destroyed the artefact before it could cause any more chaos. At the time, it had felt like barely scraping by. But compared to groups who had avoided the artefact altogether or been caught in traps, it almost sounded impressive.

Brie frowned slightly, unsure of how to feel about that. Had they been reckless? Lucky? Or had they actually done well? She wasn't used to thinking of herself as someone who excelled at these kinds of tests.

***

The rest of the day passed uneventfully – at least by Ravenscroft standards. Classes were filled with the usual mix of dull lectures and dangerous practical exercises, and Brie found herself almost enjoying the routine.

By the time evening rolled around, Brie was ready to relax. She and Melinda headed to the common room, where a small group of students was gathered around a makeshift poker table.

"Room for two more?" Melinda asked, dropping into an empty chair.

"Only if you're ready to lose," one of the players said, grinning.

"Big talk," Brie said, pulling up a chair beside Melinda. "Let's see if you can back it up."

The game was loud and animated, with spells flying as students tried to bluff or cheat their way to victory. Brie found herself laughing more than she had in weeks, her usual defences lowered in the warmth of the group.

Halfway through the game, a familiar voice cut through the noise.

"Miss Holloway."

The room fell silent as all eyes turned to the doorway, where Madam Delacroix stood with her usual air of authority.

Brie groaned internally, already bracing herself. "Yes, Headmistress?"

"A word," Madam Delacroix said, motioning for her to follow.

Brie stood, glancing at Melinda, who gave her a sympathetic shrug. "Good luck," Melinda whispered.

***

Madam Delacroix led Brie into her office, the heavy doors creaking shut behind them. The room was as imposing as ever, its dim lighting and towering bookshelves casting long shadows across the floor.

"Take a seat," Madam Delacroix said, gesturing to the chair in front of her desk.

Brie sat, her hands resting on her lap as she waited for the inevitable lecture.

Madam Delacroix sat down opposite Brie.

"You've made quite an impression since arriving at Ravenscroft," she began.

To her surprise, Madam Delacroix's tone was calm, almost... reflective.

"Uh... thanks?" Brie said cautiously.

"It wasn't a compliment," Madam Delacroix said, though her expression softened slightly. "You've tested my patience more times than I care to count, but you've also shown remarkable growth – particularly during the recent assessment."

Brie frowned. "You mean when we destroyed the artefact?"

Madam Delacroix nodded. "An unorthodox solution, but effective nonetheless. Your willingness to take risks is both your greatest strength and your greatest flaw."

Brie shifted in her seat. "So... am I in trouble, or...?"

Madam Delacroix didn't answer right away. Instead, she leaned back in her chair, studying Brie with a thoughtful expression.

It wasn't the usual cold calculation, nor was it the passive disappointment Brie had grown accustomed to receiving from authority figures. This was something different. Something almost... frank.

"What do you actually want, Miss Holloway?"

Brie blinked, caught completely off guard. "What?"

Madam Delacroix's gaze didn't waver. "What is it that you want? Beyond the posturing. Beyond the defiance. If you had your way, what would your life look like?"

Brie opened her mouth to fire back some sarcastic quip, but nothing came out. The question lodged itself in her brain, taking up space unexpectedly. She frowned, shifting in her seat. "I mean... I want to get out of here."

Madam Delacroix tilted her head, waiting for more.

"I want to prove that I'm ready to leave," Brie continued, trying to regain some of her usual edge. "That I can behave well enough to get the Magic Council's blessing to go back to my old life."

She thought that would be the end of it – that the headmistress would nod, dismiss her, maybe even tell her what hoops she'd need to jump through to convince the Magic Council she was rehabilitated or whatever nonsense they wanted from her.

But instead, Madam Delacroix simply asked, "Go back to what, exactly?"

The question hit Brie harder than she wanted to admit. What was there to go back to?

Her mind flickered to the last day of her old life – the day she'd been brought here, against her will and complaining, for the heinous crime of making some turkey taste like nail polish. She remembered standing behind the deli counter, utterly bored, slicing the same stupid cuts of meat for customers who barely acknowledged her existence. The most exciting part of the job had been figuring out how to entertain herself without getting fired.

Brie slouched slightly in her chair, her bravado faltering. Outside of Ravenscroft, her life had been... fine, she supposed. She had friends, family, and freedom, sure. But beyond that? What was there, really? A pay cheque? A never-ending loop of meaningless work and routine? Spells cast purely for the sake of amusing herself?

She'd spent so much time thinking that she didn't belong at Ravenscroft, resentful that she'd even been brought here, but for the first time, she had to admit – there hadn't been much to belong to before.

Brie exhaled, rubbing her temples. Normally, she'd shove thoughts like this aside, maybe drown them out with jokes or loud music. But something about the headmistress' stare made her feel like avoidance wasn't an option.

"I guess... I don't know," Brie admitted, surprising even herself. "I mean, my life wasn't bad, but it wasn't exactly thrilling either. I was mostly just... existing."

It felt weird, saying it out loud. Like she was betraying something. But at the same time, it felt... honest.

Madam Delacroix's expression didn't change. If she was surprised by Brie's candour, she didn't show it. Instead, she nodded as if she'd been expecting exactly this response.

"I've seen many witches like you, Miss Holloway," she said. "Gifted, but aimless. Capable, but restless. Bored of a world that does not challenge them. Some waste that potential. Others recognise it and do something with it."

Brie raised an eyebrow. "And let me guess – you think I should be doing something with it?"

Madam Delacroix steepled her fingers. "If you prove that you can change your ways – if you demonstrate to the Magic Council that you can control your impulses and act with purpose – then yes, you will be granted permission to leave Ravenscroft and return to your old life."

Brie exhaled slowly, only now realising she'd been holding her breath. That was all she needed to do? Behave?

That was doable.

"Well, that's a relief," she said, smirking as she

sat up straighter. "Guess I'll eventually start counting down the days until I can…"

"I wasn't finished," Madam Delacroix interjected smoothly.

Brie clamped her mouth shut, frowning. "There's a catch, isn't there?"

Madam Delacroix's lips twitched with the faintest hint of amusement. "Not a catch. An alternative."

Brie narrowed her eyes. "Go on."

Madam Delacroix folded her hands neatly on her desk. "Based on your performance during your time here – your handling of chaotic magic, your ability to assess high-risk situations, and your potential in spellcraft – I would be willing to recommend you for a mentorship."

Brie blinked. "A what?"

Madam Delacroix met her stare evenly. "If you prove yourself – truly prove yourself – I will put your name forward for a Magic Council mentorship. You would leave

Ravenscroft and train at a specialist academy that prepares witches to work for the Magic Council."

Brie stared at her, the words taking an absurdly long time to sink in.

Madam Delacroix remained impassive.

"I... wait..." Brie said, surprised and a little confused. "You're telling me... you think I should be part of the Magic Council? Me? The person who hexed a customer's food out of pure spite?"

Brie smirked at the memory, but the expression quickly faded as she thought back to all the little spells she'd used over the years – petty, harmless things that had amused her in the moment but never had any real purpose. Spells to make food taste weird, to turn off security cameras when she was sneaking out of work early, to change the expiration dates on milk cartons just to mess with people.

She'd never once thought of her magic as something truly useful.

Brie forced herself to sit up straighter, rubbing a hand over her face. "Ok, but wait. If I do this mentorship thing, does that mean I'd have to arrest other witches and bring them here?"

Madam Delacroix inclined her head. "That may be part of it, yes."

Brie wrinkled her nose. "Yeah, I'm not keen on that idea. Seems a bit too authoritarian for my liking."

Madam Delacroix regarded her carefully. "Then think about it this way: being sent here has served to help you, has it not?"

Brie opened her mouth, ready to argue, but stopped. The headmistress had a point. The idea of having a plan for her life had never crossed her mind. She was so used to living impulsively. The thought of choosing a path felt almost too big, too overwhelming to comprehend.

"Can I think about it?" Brie asked after a long moment.

Madam Delacroix regarded her with a steady gaze. "Of course," she said, her tone softer than usual. "I urge you to consider this conversation carefully."

Brie swallowed, absorbing the weight of the words.

Madam Delacroix's expression shifted back to its usual, impassive form. With a small wave of her hand, she gestured to the door. "You are dismissed."

Brie nodded stiffly and made her way out, her thoughts racing as she walked back towards the common room. She had never cared much about planning for her future, but now that someone had put the idea in her head, she wasn't so sure she could ignore it anymore.

Epilogue

Eight months later, Madam Delacroix and the other professors finally decided that Brie had served her time at Ravenscroft – eight months of learning, struggling, rolling her eyes at authority, and, of course, getting involved in *just a little* chaos.

The length of time wasn't a surprise to Brie – she had known from the start that she wasn't the kind of student who would suddenly morph into a model witch overnight. And besides, she wouldn't have wanted that anyway. Ravenscroft may have been a reformatory, but for Brie, it had been something else: it had been *fun*.

That was largely thanks to Melinda, whose never-ending ability to create mayhem had kept Brie entertained even when she probably should have been focusing on self-improvement. Whether it was sneaking enchanted frogs into the potions lab or hexing Charmina's quill to change her handwriting into something ugly, Melinda had been a constant source of trouble – and Brie had happily gone along for the ride.

The difference was, Brie knew when to stop.

At least, she *eventually* figured it out.

She'd learnt the fine art of picking her battles, of knowing when to push the rules and when to follow them. She still got into trouble sometimes, but it gradually became less frequent.

Charmina still carried herself like she was a shining example of discipline, still talked down to students who didn't meet her exacting standards, and still acted like rules were something sacred. But with Brie, since she had apologised after the assessment in the portal that day, she had been respectful. They weren't friends, not by a long shot, but they'd reached a silent agreement to stay out of each other's way. Brie was fine with that. She was even happy for Charmina when she was granted her exit date from Ravenscroft. It made sense – Charmina had been there longer, and while her attitude was still unpleasant in many ways, she was clearly ready to move on with her life.

By the time her own release date arrived, Brie had changed more than she'd expected to. It wasn't just that she wanted out; she wanted to move forward. In the months leading up to her release, she had spent a long time unsure about whether to take up Madam Delacroix's offer of a mentorship, teetering between her old habits and the possibility of something bigger. In classic Brie fashion, she hadn't followed a neat, linear path to good behaviour. She'd *tried* to be on her best behaviour, only to get caught up in mischief in one way or another. She'd *attempted* to keep her rebellious streak in check, only to realise that sometimes, rebellion wasn't about being difficult – it was about questioning things that needed to be questioned.

But eventually, she came to a decision.

She didn't just want to *leave* Ravenscroft. She wanted to leave with a plan. She wanted to have a future where she wasn't just floating through life, casting petty spells out of boredom. She wanted to see what she was capable of when she actually tried.

Melinda, however, was *not* getting out anytime soon.

It wasn't surprising – Melinda had zero interest in playing by the rules long enough to get permission to leave. She treated Ravenscroft as a playground for her endless pranks, and as long as she was still entertained, she wasn't in any rush. Brie couldn't say she agreed, but she respected it. More than that, she would always appreciate Melinda's friendship.

No one had stood by her like Melinda had. When the academy had been overwhelming, suffocating even, Melinda had made it bearable. She'd made Brie laugh when she wanted to scream, had given her something to look forward to when she felt stuck. Brie wasn't surprised that Melinda was yet to be granted a leaving date, but she hoped that one day, the mischievous witch would take the necessary steps to make it happen.

Not long after Brie left Ravenscroft, word reached her that Lisa had been given her release date. Lisa had learnt her lesson – she wasn't going to mess around with magic beyond her capabilities again. Brie had no doubt that when Lisa stepped back into the outside world, she'd stay on the straight and narrow. For all the mistakes she'd made, Lisa had never wanted to be a troublemaker. She'd just got in over her head. Brie was happy for her.

When Brie passed her final exams at Ravenscroft, Madam Delacroix didn't hesitate to recommend her for the mentorship programme with the Magic Council.

Brie noticed straight away that the mentorship academy was different from Ravenscroft. It wasn't a reform academy. The witches training there were learning how to use their magic for a greater purpose – to help others, to maintain balance, to keep watch over witches who needed guidance. Brie still wasn't sure how she felt about all of it. The idea of enforcing rules still didn't sit right with her, but she also couldn't deny that *some* rules existed for a reason. If someone had told her a year ago that she'd be here, learning how to be part of the system that had once dragged her kicking and screaming into a reformatory, she would have hexed them on the spot.

But now she had the chance to use her skills for something useful. She had a purpose, and for the first time in her life, she had things to look forward to. That didn't mean she'd lost who she was. Her hair was still green. Her sarcasm was still sharp. Her humour was still dark.

She was *still Brie*.

Just... a Brie who no longer felt like she had to rebel *just* to feel alive. A Brie who had learnt that maybe, just maybe, the Magic Council had done her a favour by dragging her to Ravenscroft that fateful day. Because honestly? What an amazing – albeit challenging – experience it had been.

And what a story she'd have to tell.